Bus-a-Saurus Bop

To Nathan,
Have a boppin'
good time!

Diane Shore
2009

For John, Jenn, and Sam, who helped make it all happen
—D.Z.S.

For Betsy
—D.C.

Text copyright © 2003 by Diane Z. Shore
Illustrations copyright © 2003 by David Clark
Type set in Imperfect
The art was done in pen and ink and watercolor
Designed by Carl J. Ferrero

Published by Bloomsbury, New York and London
Distributed to the trade by Holtzbrinck Publishers, LLC
Library of Congress Cataloging-in-Publication Data
Shore, Diane ZuHone.
Bus-a-saurus Bop / by Diane ZuHone Shore; David Clark, [illustrator]. p. cm.
Summary: A boy describes his school bus as a big yellow monster
that gobbles up students and takes them to school.
ISBN 1-58234-850-2 (alk. paper)
[1. School buses—Fiction. 2. Stories in rhyme.] I. Clark, David, ill. II. Title.
PZ8.3.S55918 Bu 2003
[E]—dc21
2002028339

First U.S. Edition 2003
4 5 6 7 8 9 10

BLOOMSBURY
CHILDREN'S
BOOKS

Bloomsbury USA Children's Books
175 Fifth Avenue
New York, NY 10010

BUS-A-SAURUS BOP

by Diane Z. Shore
illustrated by David Clark

BLOOMSBURY
CHILDREN'S
BOOKS

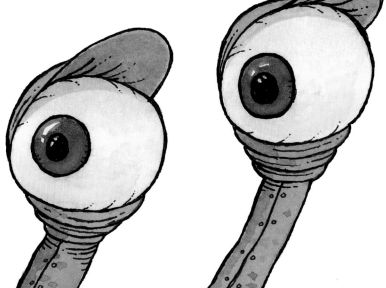

Early in the mornin'
when the sun is done a-snorin',
the boppin' bus-a-saurus
comes a-rippin' and a-roarin'.

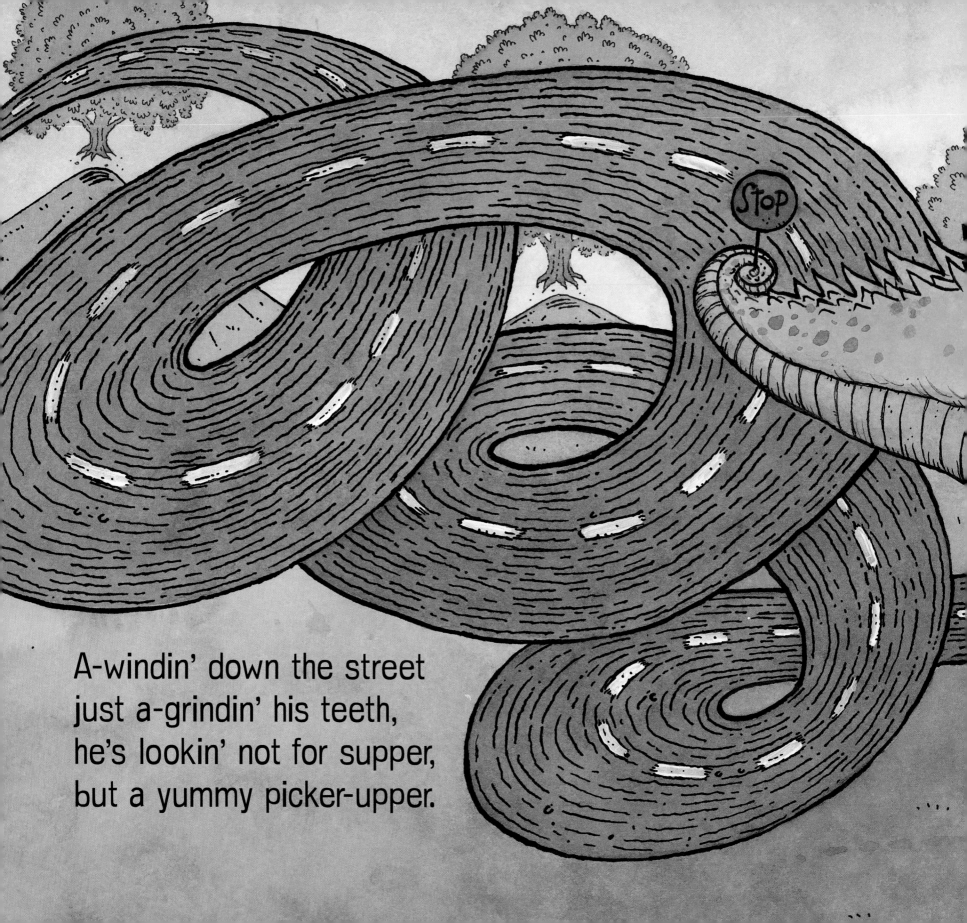

A-windin' down the street
just a-grindin' his teeth,
he's lookin' not for supper,
but a yummy picker-upper.

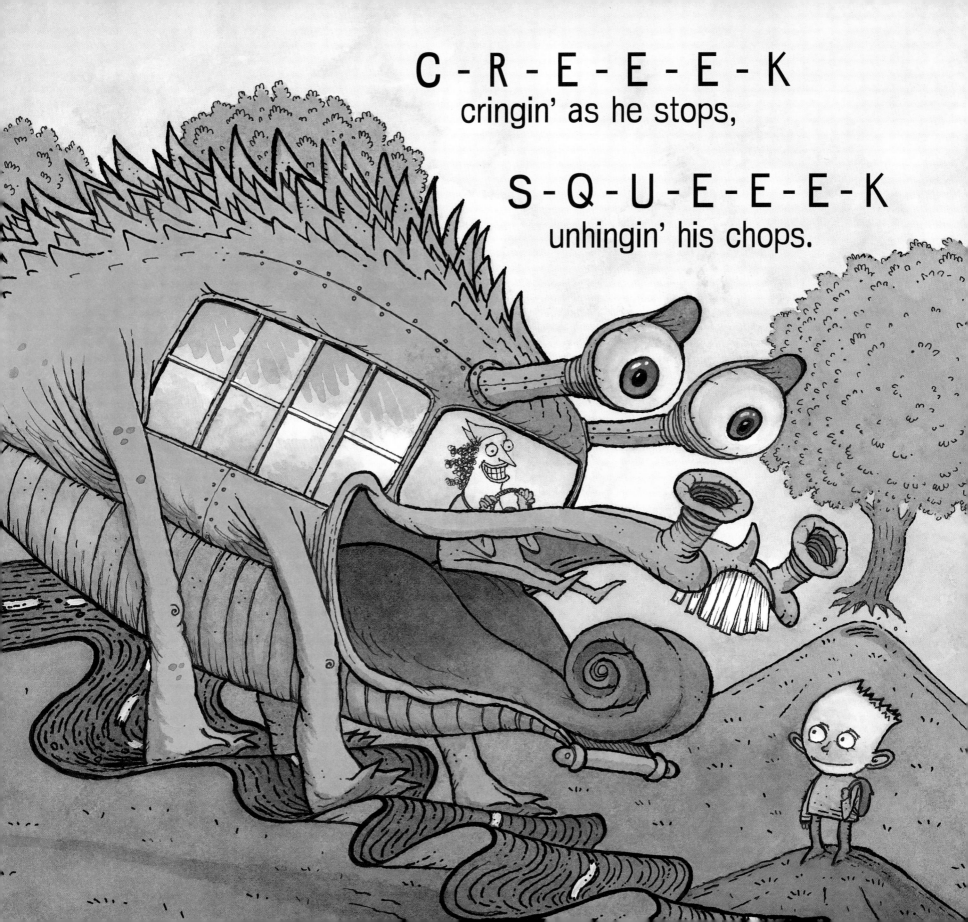

Then he mumble rumble grumbles as I
STOMP! STOMP! STOMP!
up the steps with clompy feet,
where Miss Hopper in her seat
tells me "Mornin', Mr. Norman,"
then I . . .

ROMP! ROMP! ROMP!
to my buddies in the back
where I park it next to Zack
deep inside the bus-a-saurus
as he CHOMP! CHOMP! CHOMPS!

Now he closes up his chops,
but he has a few more stops.
So we're boppin' in his belly
just a-jigglin' like jelly
'til he bops around to gobble Lotta Tott.

Then Lotta dances to her seat,
just a-boppin' to the beat
with her ponytail a-swingin'
and her hair barrettes a-springin'
deep inside the bus-a-saurus as he
CHOMP! CHOMP! CHOMPS!

Now we're boppin' and a-poppin'
and a-floppin' off to Flip's,
and a-rockin' round to Robin's,
and a-truckin' down to Trip's.

Then he peeks around a corner
'round a curvy cul-de-sac,
on the lookout for a
munchy-crunchy snack.

C-R-E-E-E-K
cringin' as he stops,

S-Q-U-E-E-E-K
unhingin' his chops,
but the Tardee Twins
are nowhere to be seen...
BEEP! BEEP!

Now they're boundin' out the door,
like they did the day before,
with their backpacks flippy-flappin,'

and their puppy yippy-yappin'
as they charge across the yard
and barge on board.

"P - U - P - P - Y ! !"
Miss Hopper hollers, "STOP HER!"
as the puppy hops on top her
then a-bounces and a-pounces
on my lap.

And the kids are all a-rootin',
and Miss Hopper's nearly hootin',
'cause the puppy's tickle-lickin'
me and Zack.

Then the bus-a-saurus snuffles
and a-huffles and a-puffles
so I whisk the puppy off
and come on back.

S-L-U-R-P!
He closes up his chops,
'cause he's gobbled all his stops,
so he winds around
and grinds on down the street.

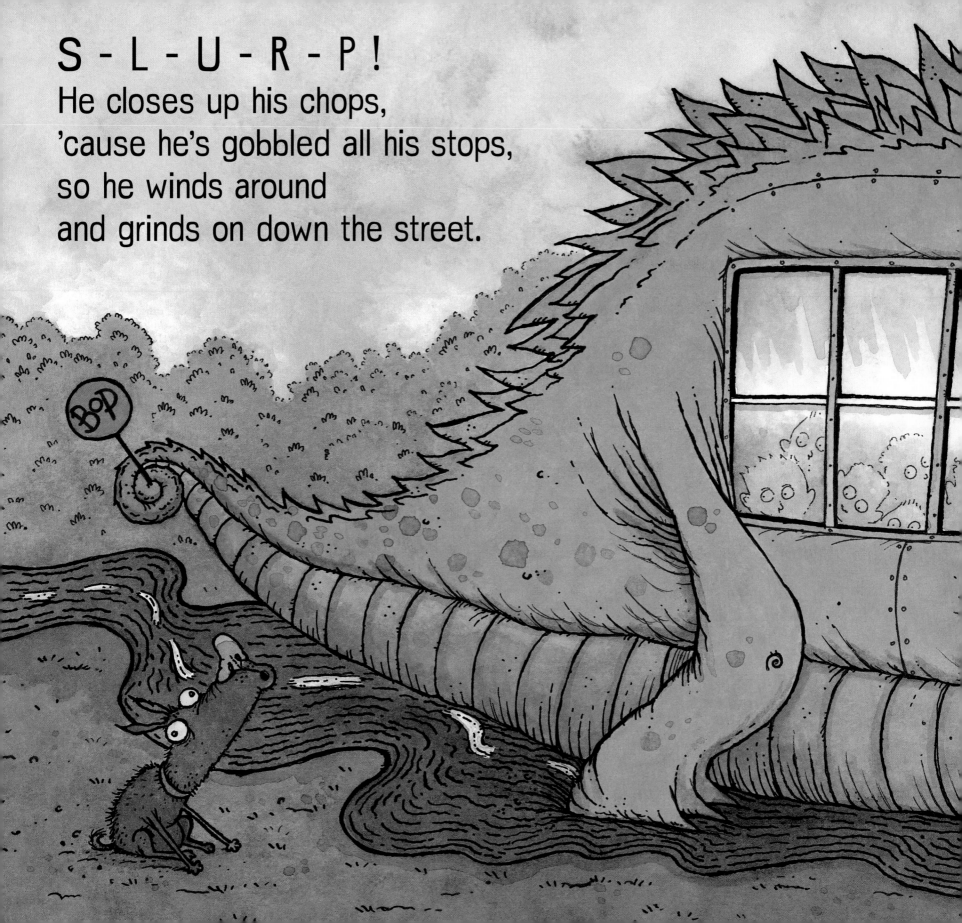

Now we're scootin' on to school
'cause his tummy's plenty full.
Oh, he's moanin' and a-groanin'
and so slowly he's a-rollin'
just a-chuggin' and a-luggin'
up the lane.

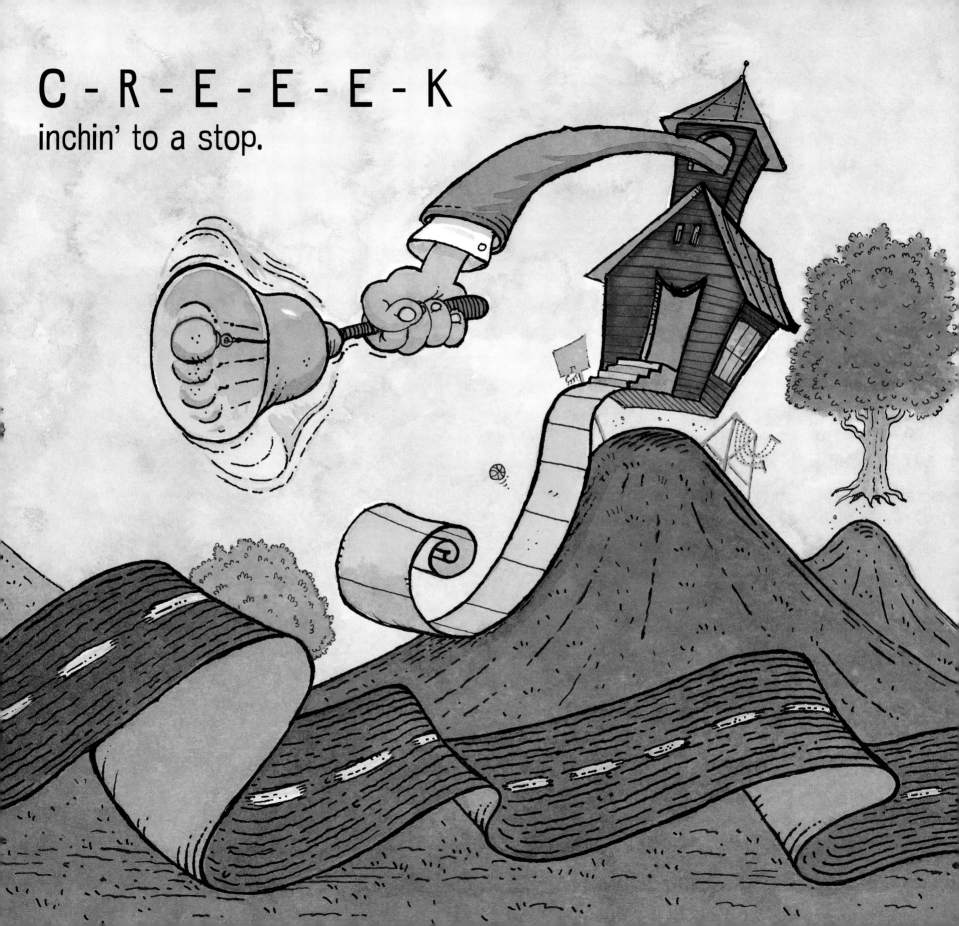

S - Q - U - E - E - E - K
unhingin' his chops,
then he hisses out a mountain of a burp—
Shhh-ERRRP!

Now he's spewin' like a fountain
as about and out we're spoutin',
just a-shoutin' and a-crowdin'
down the steps.

As we're skippin' and a-trippin'
and a-zippin' into school,
he starts to feelin' spunky,
not so chunky, clunky, lunky,

'cause his tummy's not so
puffy-stuffy full.
S - L - U - R - P
he closes up his chops
for he's polished off his stops,

so he rumbles and he grumbles
down the lane.
But he always bumbles back
for an afternooner snack,

which he bobble-gobbles down,
then he wobbles back around,
and he burps us out reversed,
with the Tardees goin' first...

and the rest of us in spurts around the town!

Woof!

WOOF!